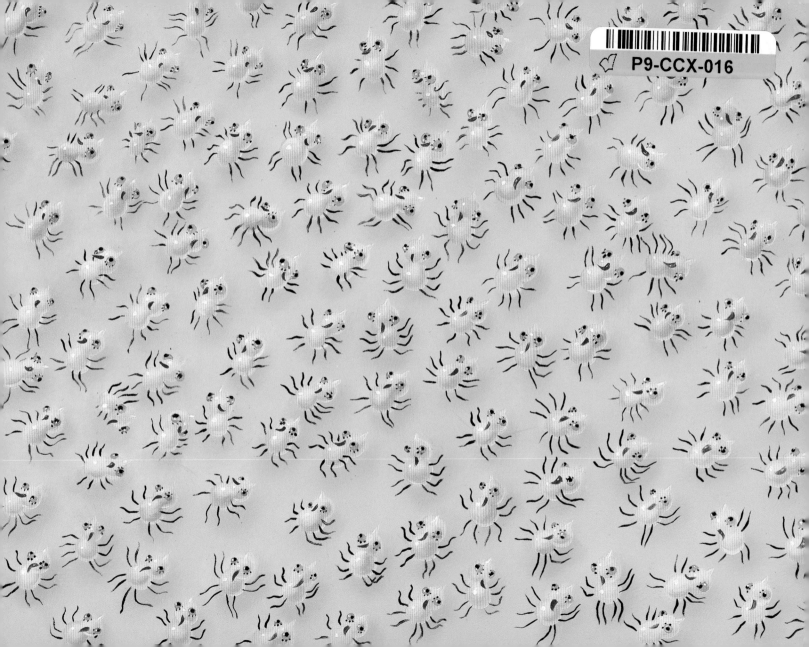

For my Moliet

Nicholas Callaway, Editorial Director
Antoinette White, Senior Editor · Toshiya Masuda, Designer · True Sims, Production Director
Paula Litzky, Director of Sales & Marketing · Monica Moran, Director of Publicity
Jeremy Ross, Director of New Technology · Christopher Steighner, Assistant Editor
Ivan Wong, Jr. and José Rodríguez, Design & Production Associates
With thanks to Priya Nair at Scholastic Press and to Debbie Geri and Raphael Shea.

Library of Congress Cataloging-in-Publication Data
Kirk, David, 1955–
Little Miss Spider / paintings and verse by David Kirk.
p. cm.
Summary: On her very first day of life, Little Miss Spider searches for her mother and finds love in an unexpected place.
ISBN 0-439-08389-3
[1. Spiders—Fiction. 2. Insects—Fiction. 3. Mother and child—Fiction. 4. Stories in rhyme.]
I. Title.
PZ8.3.K6554LI                          1999
[E]—dc21                          98-49270
CIP                          AC
10 9 8 7 6 5 4 3 2 1   9/9 0/0 1 2 3 4

Printed in Hong Kong by Palace Press International
First edition, October 1999

The paintings in this book are oils on paper.

# Little Miss Spider

paintings and verse by David Kirk

Scholastic Press

Callaway

New York

Little Miss Spider
Popped out of her egg.
Swinging down from a thread,
She hung on by one leg.

Watching brothers and sisters
All scooting for cover,
She dangled there wondering,
"Where is my mother?"

"Did she squeeze down a hole?
Or dive underwater?
Why won't she come out here
And meet her new daughter?"

She climbed to the
Tippity-top of a tree.
Gazing out on the world,
She sobbed, "Where could Mom be?"

A beetle named Betty
Buzzed by this high perch.
"A child needs a mother.
May I please help you search?"

"I don't know for sure,
But I'll offer this clue —
If I were your mom,
I'd be looking for you."

They flew through the trees,
Spying down from the sky,
And asked all the butterflies
Fluttering by.

But none of the insects
They happened upon
Had any idea
Where her mother had gone.

She then asked a small spider –
As plump as a pig! –
"Have *you* seen my mom?
She's like me, only big."

The sly spider laughed
As he gobbled his snack,
"Up there is a mother
Who's yellow and black."

With a heart full of joy,
She peered over the straw,
But it wasn't her mother
That Miss Spider saw. . . .

It was six hungry hatchlings
And a goldfinch, who cried,
"Your dinner's here darlings,
So open up wide!"

Before she could blink,
She was whisked out of sight,
And brave beetle Betty
Was hugging her tight.

In her warm cozy home
In the bark of a tree,
The kind beetle asked,
"Won't you stay here with me?"

Then Miss Spider smiled,
And held Betty fast.
"I looked for my mom,
And I found you at last."

For finding your mother,
There's one certain test.
You must look for the creature
Who loves you the best.